To my son Alix
V. d'H.

To Anto, have a good trip!
L. B.

Text © 2006 Laurence Bourguignon
Illustrations © 2006 Valérie d'Heur
Published in 2008 by Eerdmans Books for Young Readers,
an imprint of Wm. B. Eerdmans Publishing Co.

First published by Mijade in Belgium in 2006

Wm. B. Eerdmans Publishing Co.
2140 Oak Industrial Dr. NE, Grand Rapids, Michigan 49505
P.O. Box 163, Cambridge CB3 9PU U.K.

www.eerdmans.com/youngreaders

Printed in Belgium

14 13 12 11 10 09 08   8 7 6 5 4 3 2 1

Library of Congress Cataloging-in-Publication Data

Bourguignon, Laurence.
[Coeur dans la poche. English]
Heart in the pocket / by Laurence Bourguignon ; illustrated by
Valerie d'Heur.
p. cm.
Summary: A baby kangaroo is reluctant to leave the comfort of
his mother's pocket, where he is safe and warm and can always
hear her heartbeat — until he finds out that her heart is not
actually in her pocket.

ISBN 978-0-8028-5343-1 (alk. paper)

[1. Kangaroos — Fiction. 2. Animals — Infancy — Fiction. 3.
Mother and child — Fiction.] I. Heur, Valérie d', ill. II. Title.
PZ7.B6656He 2008
[E]—dc22
                                        2007049348

Heart in the Pocket

written by

Laurence Bourguignon

illustrated by

Valérie d'Heur

Eerdmans Books for Young Readers

Grand Rapids, Michigan • Cambridge, U.K.

Mama Kangaroo loves her little Jo-Jo a lot, lot, lot.

She sings him sweet songs.
She gives him beautiful
desert flowers.
And she gently rocks
him to sleep in her pocket.

Mama shows Jo-Jo all the
beauties of the desert.

The wild wind
dancing in the sand.
A small bird nesting
in the mahogany tree.
A butterfly gliding on
the breeze.
And a floating cloud in the
blue, blue sky.

"Wouldn't you like to be a floating cloud?" Mama asks.
"Not me," Jo-Jo says. "The wild wind will blow that cloud far away. I want to stay in your pocket, where I'm safe and warm!"

"But if you were the wild wind," says Mama, "you could travel far and wide. You could see things that you have never seen before."

"Oh no," says Jo-Jo. "The wind is always blowing. It never stops to rest, and it doesn't have a home. I want to stay in your pocket, where I can sleep and dream whenever I want."

"You could be a bird," Mama says.
"Birds are free and can fly far, far away.
But they can always come home to their
cozy nests high in the mahogany trees."

"Oh no," Jo-Jo says. "A nest isn't soft and warm, like your pocket is. And your pocket jumps, dances, and rocks me to sleep."

"What about a butterfly?" Mama asks.
"Butterflies are soft and ever so light.
They float on the breeze and know how
to find the prettiest desert flowers."

"Mama, you know where all the flowers are!" says Jo-Jo. "And you know how to find water hidden in the desert, and the green, green grass that we love to eat. I want to stay in your pocket, so we can do everything together!"

"Hmmm," says Mama. "What if you were a lizard?"

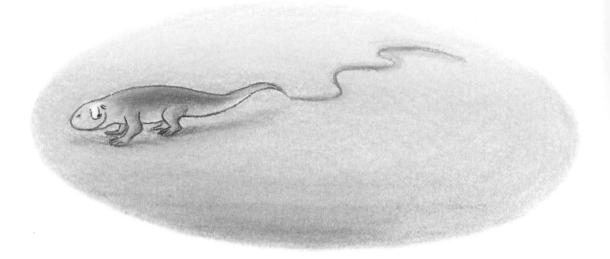

"You could draw rivers and birds and flowers in the sand with your long lizard tail."

"I can already draw. Look!"

Jo-Jo leans out of the pocket and uses
a big stick to make a figure in the sand.

"See, it's a mama kangaroo with a baby in her pocket. The baby will stay in the pocket forever so he can always hear his mama's heartbeat."

"Ah, I see. My little Jo-Jo,
did you know that my heart is not
in my pocket? My heart is up here,"
Mama says, pointing to her chest.
"If you climb a little higher, you
will hear it beating."

Jo-Jo slowly creeps out of the pocket.
Then he stands on his tippy-toes and
falls right into his mother's arms.

"There you are, my little kangaroo! See, it's not so bad outside the pocket!"

Mama kisses his nose, his eyes, his chin, all the fingers on both hands, and Jo-Jo's two big funny feet.

Jo-Jo giggles. "Put me down, Mama!"

Mama gently places him on the sandy ground.
The wild wind blows.
The birds sing in the mahogany trees.
The butterflies dance on the breeze.
But there isn't a cloud in sight.

"Where did the clouds go?" Jo-Jo asks.
"Far, far away, little one."
"Let's go chase them!"
And they leapt with the wind across the sand.

Mama Kangaroo loves her Jo-Jo a lot, lot, lot.
She sings him sweet songs.
She finds him beautiful desert flowers.

And she will always hold his heart in her pocket.